Disintegration

&

Other

Stories

By Paula Acton

Also By This Author

Voices Across The Void

Ascension: Queen Of Ages

Trilogy Book 1

All characters and events in this publication are fictitious and any resemblance to actual persons, living or dead, is purely coincidental.

This book is sold subject to the conditions that it shall not, by way of trade or otherwise, be lent, resold,
hired out or otherwise circulated without the author's prior written consent
in any form of binding or cover other
than that in which it is published
and without a similar condition being
imposed upon the subsequent purchaser.

Copyright ©2015 by Paula Acton

The moral right of the author has been asserted.

Contents

Dedication 1

Disintegration 3

Saturday 3

Sunday 10

Monday 19

Tuesday 23

Wednesday 27

Thursday 31

Final Disintegration 35

Broken 39

What The Sleeping Hear 41

The Black Sheep 50

TABLE FOR ONE 58

Karma in Oils 66

DEUCE 72

ONE LAST TIME 82

Empty 90

Author's Notes 98

About The Author 99

Paula Acton

Dedication

This collection of short stories is dedicated to my grandma Edna May Callis who passed away 26th January 2015 aged 90. She was one of the strongest women I have ever had the honour of knowing, she taught me so many things but the most important was that you do not have to choose between your dreams and your family, you just have to put the same amount of effort into each.

Paula Acton

Disintegration

Saturday

It started on a Saturday.

Well that's not quite true it must have been there festering away before then, but that's when I became aware of it. The previous night we had sat curled up together on the sofa watching War of the Roses, maybe that is where he got the idea. As we watched Kathleen Turner swing from the chandelier, I made a joke about how it would not have the same effect swinging from a single bulb light fitting, he laughed and countered that it was a good job neither of us had pets. We had finished the bottle of wine then headed to bed, he cuddled up to me but I was exhausted and no sooner had my head hit the pillow than I was fast asleep, I awoke to find he had moved to the opposite side of the bed.

I had to go into work that morning, so I was not in the best of moods to start with, but I had no idea as I headed down the stairs what was waiting for me. I dashed about grabbing what I needed whilst trying to drink my coffee before it turned to a cold stagnant pool in my cup. I greeted him as he walked past me straight to the fridge, not even a grunt in response but he never was a morning person. He leaned in, pulled out the milk and began drinking straight from the full bottle.

"Don't do that, it's gross!"

He stopped, turned, and glared at me. It always seemed to be the little things we argued over, and even then, it was more sniping than an all-out row that could be made up after. Since he had been laid off a couple of months before there seemed to be more and more little things.

"If you don't like it, leave!"

I stopped in my tracks and turned to face him unable to believe I had heard him correctly.

"Pardon?"

"You heard me if I annoy you so much… there's the door use it."

I shook my head; it seemed every morning as I set off to work it was becoming more like a war zone. His resentment at me having a job to go to was displayed as I prepared to depart, a couple of times I even suspected he had deliberately hidden the car keys, or moved my phone, in an attempt to undermine my confidence before I headed off on days I had mentioned were going to be stressful already. I grabbed my bag and keys then headed to the door, pausing at the threshold.

"You want to be careful one day I might just do that and not come back."

I walked out slamming the door behind me so hard that I froze for a moment scared the glass would shatter. I reached the car but as I tried to put the key in the ignition my hands were shaking so badly it took several attempts before the engine roared into life. As I backed out of the drive, I thought for a moment I saw the blinds move and imagined him gloating over the fact he had upset me.

The journey to work passed in a blur, thankfully it was quiet on the roads that morning. I stopped off and grabbed a coffee, they knew me well enough that I didn't need to string the words together to order, smiles and nods were all that were needed to complete the journey,

I had tried to be understanding, I really had, but my patience was wearing thin. I sat at my desk staring at the picture of us together, trying to work out why it was going wrong. We had met, fallen in love and married within months, everyone said I was a fool to rush things. But I just knew he was the one. He had a good job, a house and was a wonderful guy, what more could a girl want. Okay, so I did earn more than him, but it had never mattered until now. The house was still in his name, we had never gotten round to changing it after all we were going to be together for ever, so what did it matter. I paid the mortgage, I had since we moved in until he lost his job, he paid all the other bills gradually they began drifting from his account to mine but what did it matter we were a couple.

I remembered the first time I had seen him, we were in the coffee shop across from where I work, I was already sat at a table, people watching from behind a magazine, as he stood at the counter placing his order. I had watched him from a distance, each lunch time it seemed I would arrive before him and take my seat then he would come in and order his to go. It had seemed like he had never noticed me watching him, then one day he looked straight into my eyes and I melted as I ducked behind the magazine to cover my blushes. The next day we made eye contact again, this time I managed a smile and as he returned it, I noticed he had the cutest dimples that formed in his cheeks.

The next day he broke from routine and joined me at the table, we had spent every lunchtime together from then right up until him losing his job.

The first sign I had when I returned that evening that something was wrong was the delicious smells coming from the kitchen. He never cooked.

As I walked in, I saw the table piled high with a disturbing amount of different foods. Then I noticed it. A line dissected the kitchen floor. Thick silver duct tape. He stood by the table I looked at him quizzically.

"This is my side and that is yours."

I let out a laugh, he couldn't possibly be serious.

"I told you to leave this morning but as you didn't listen, I am going to spell it out for you. I want my life back. Since I met you everything has gone wrong. So, if you refuse to leave, you will live by my rules under MY roof."

"Okay…"

By this point I was beginning to get a little concerned, this wasn't funny, but I still could not believe he was serious. I knew he had got the idea from the film last night, but this was madness, he was obviously having some sort of meltdown. I decided for tonight at least I would humour him, we were both stressed out and arguing right now would only make things worse.

"I suppose you had better tell me what your rules are then."

"You stay in your assigned areas; I stay in mine. You do not touch or use anything in my side. You have half the kitchen; I have the other half. I get the living room; you get the dining room. I keep MY bedroom with the en-suite, you get the spare room and use the house bathroom."

I opened my mouth to protest but he continued.

"I have already moved your stuff out of my areas and placed it in yours."

He spoke with such bitterness I could no longer fool myself he was joking. I felt the tears begin to well up in my eyes, determined not to cry in front of him I ran from the room. Automatically I headed to our bedroom but as I passed the spare bedroom I stopped and looked in.

All my belongings lay on the floor discarded, a lid had come off a bottle of lotion, white cream splattered and smeared amongst them. Clothes were piled on the bed, shoes, make up and other possessions formed a mountain in the corner of the room. I could not bring myself to look any closer.

I threw myself down on the bed and crawled down amongst the clothes until eventually I cried myself to sleep.

Sunday

It was still dark when I awoke, I fought against the items which were wrapped around me, panicking, before I realised it was simply clothing binding me. It took a few minutes for me to get my bearings and remember where I was.

I lay in the dark, contemplating what had happened. He was angry and bitter and that was obviously the cause of him acting like an arse. No doubt he expected me to go creeping along the corridor to our room. Expected me to slide into bed next to him grovelling and apologetic, well bollocks to him. He would have a long wait.

I realised I was starving; I hadn't eaten when I got in due to his little drama queen performance. I got up and felt my way to the wall, stumbling over shoes and bags before I groped my way to the light switch.

Damn! Just as the light came on my foot descended on the open lotion. A thick glob of cream shot from the bottle landing in the middle of a new trouser suit I had bought for a meeting at work on Monday.

Cursing I scooped it up, along with a few other items soiled by the errant cream. I made a mental note to take an inventory of all the things that had been ruined by his stupidity. I still did not think that he was really serious, but I was hungry, tired and annoyed, and determined to think no more until I had consumed at least one cup of coffee.

I set off towards the kitchen clutching the soiled trouser suit. I planned it out in my head that if I put them in the washer with a pre-soak now and turned it on as soon as it reached a reasonable hour, I would still have time to dry and press the suit, and wear it still tomorrow. I was about three feet from the washing machine when he spoke.

"You are on my side of the room."

I stopped and looked round, he was sat in the far corner of the room, he had been hidden by the door as I had entered.

"Are you really going to keep this up?"

"If you don't like it, you can leave."

"Whatever!"

I turned and looked at the floor then stepped back across the silver dividing line. I dropped my clothes in a pile, for the minute, there was nothing I could do with them.

For the first time now, I took stock of his division of our space. The table sat directly across the central line, one chair on my side, one on his. He had even gone so far as to stripe the table with the tape, ensuring that it matched the floor, as if he believed we would sit facing one another, it made me think of a prison visitors table like the ones you saw on TV shows. I wondered how long he had spent while I had been at work the day before measuring the halfway point.

His side contained the fridge, washing machine, dishwasher, and cooker. I had been left with the freezer, most of the cupboards, the microwave, and the sink. My head now started pounding, I reached into my handbag which still lay where I had put it on the table when I had returned home the day before and pulled out some painkillers. I opened the cupboard to reach for a glass to get some water, nothing.

The cupboard was bare. I opened the next, again empty. Then I noticed the stack of boxes piled in the corner, the idiot had actually gone to the trouble of removing every single cup, glass and plate from the cupboards and piled them up in the boxes on his side of the kitchen. I leaned over the sink and stuck my head under the tap slurping at the running water.

I stood at the sink looking out of the window when a realisation struck me. The food he had been cooking when I got home yesterday… I could hear him laughing as I walked to look at the contents of the freezer. Empty, the stupid git must have spent the whole day while I was at work cooking everything he could. I turned and looked at him, he was now stood by the fridge and slowly opened the door to reveal the overstuffed shelves.

"Okay you want to play it that way, fine! But let me tell you, you are way out of your league!"

I turned and headed to the dining room. Sitting at the table I began to formulate my revenge on him. I would teach him. Who the hell did he think he was? So, things hadn't been going his way, it wasn't as if he was on the verge of being homeless, I knew he felt bad about not working but that was no excuse for this crap. I would make him come begging on his knees.

As soon as the shop opened, I went around there for supplies. Paper plates, plastic cups, and cutlery, plenty of pop, biscuits, arms full of snacks and crap that didn't require his precious fridge. Next stop was the laundrette, I dropped off the suit and a bag full of other stuff that had been contaminated by the lotion explosion. I could collect it in the morning on my way to work and change there.

I was by now feeling rather proud of myself that despite all his plans I had not turned into the begging wreck he obviously expected me to. I walked back into the kitchen and unloaded my shopping into the cupboards. I had stopped off and picked up a coffee on my way back from my errands, that was one situation I would have to resolve, the kettle was on his side but even if it had been on mine no way could I drink my coffee black. I grabbed a can of pop, a packet of biscuits and turned on my heels.

Now for the next stage.

I had always hated the dining room. He had decorated it before I moved in, it was the one room I had not got round to transforming, I attacked the wallpaper with relish. A sense of satisfaction permeated my soul as I ripped strip after strip from the wall.

Now there would be no choice but to redecorate, I had already seen the colour scheme I wanted. He had dismissed it as garish but if he kept up this stupid game, he would have no say, it would be done before I even contemplated breaking down.

It was now mid-afternoon, and I was hot and sweaty from my exertions. As I walked past him in the hallway towards the bathroom, I noticed him looking at me, it was as if he were trying to solve a complicated maths problem. I could literally hear the cogs turning, but obviously judging from the scowl which crossed his face he did not like the answer he was coming up with.

As I slid into the warm water, I considered my next move. There was no way I was going to roll over and beg. He would be the one to come crawling, and I would make damn sure he did.

I must confess I was annoyed with myself over the dining room, while it had felt good I knew it had been a childish move, and I was frustrated I had allowed him to provoke me into doing such a foolish thing.

As I came out of the bathroom to make my way back to the bedroom, he was there again stood in the hallway watching. I pulled the towel tighter as I passed him and shut the door behind me. That would be his downfall, the one thing he could never turn down, my body.

I rooted amongst my belongings until I found what I was looking for. I sat on the edge of the bed and applied my makeup first. As I looked in the mirror, I realised that for this to work it needed more and reached to the bottom of the makeup bag.

I retrieved the bright red lipstick I had worn for a fancy-dress party when I had dressed as a

Spanish Flamenco dancer. I ran my tongue over my lips pleased with the results.

Ten minutes later I examined my appearance in the mirror. I let out a groan as I took in the outfit. He had bought me it for Christmas. I remembered the effort it had taken to smile as I lifted it from its box.

The red corset with black lace and piping was a perfect fit, I had to give him credit for that, but that was where it ended, that he ever thought this was the type of thing I would choose showed how little he paid attention. It would be ironic if his own present was his Achilles heel. I adjusted the black fishnet stockings and slipped my feet into my black stilettos.

I peeked into the hallway. He was no longer there. I drew myself up to full height then sashayed down to the kitchen. He was at the table when I entered, I ignored the spluttering as he choked on his food.

Moving over to the freezer I made to grab something from the carriers I had dumped there when I returned from my morning excursion. I accidentally on purpose knocked the contents over so they spilled across the floor.

Carefully, positioning myself for maximum effect, I bent at the waist taking my time to gather them together. I could hear him shuffling in his seat, I smiled as I turned slightly so my ass was aimed directly at him.

The next thing I heard was the sound of footsteps as he ran up the stairs. I stood up quickly banging my head against the side of the freezer as I did. Furious did not even come close to how I felt. I stood dressed like a cheap hooker as I heard him move around above my head. Then I heard the shower running. So, I had been right about his weakness, I had just failed to realise he had an escape route.

The sound of the running water echoed through my head, then I realised he had the washer running, his favourite football shirt sloshing around in the soapy water.

Water I hated that word.

Then inspiration.

The sink. I had the sink on my side.

I opened the door and sank to my knees; I pulled the cleaning products out of the way. There it was, an ally against his madness. I grabbed hold of the stopcock with both hands and twisted. Tighter and tighter.

I heard cursing from above as his shower slowed to a dribble then stopped. I looked across at the washing machine smugly, knowing that the rinse cycle would never complete. I hoped that the machine would stop itself, unable to finish filling, and his precious shirt would be trapped in there until it rotted.

Satisfied he would realise he had met his match, I decided to turn in. I was confident by the time I got home from work tomorrow he would have seen sense and the tape across the kitchen would be gone.

As I passed our bedroom door I looked in, it was open only a few inches, but I could see him reflected in the mirror trying to rub the shampoo out of his hair with a towel.

Monday

I woke up feeling strangely calm. Overnight something had clicked in my head and now it was in charge, not my foolish heart. I did not choose this, he had, but it would be up to me to bring him to his senses.

I briefly considered calling a doctor, maybe it was some sort of breakdown he was having, but he did seem terribly lucid.

If he had been delusional, well, hearing voices type delusional, not mad duct tape man, then I could have called and got someone out to see him, but I wasn't sure that wanting to divide a house in half after watching someone do it in a film actually constituted madness.

I bounced down the hallway and jumped in the shower, only remembering I had shut the water off after standing expectantly under the nozzle for a few seconds.

I considered my options, I could go down and turn it back on but hell, why bother, I would shower at the gym, I had time for a quick workout before picking my suit up and I was sure that an hour spent slogging away on the treadmill would help me clear my head and focus on what I needed to do.

An hour later, exhilarated from the treadmill, my suit collected from the laundrette cleaned and freshly pressed hanging over my arm, I stepped into my office. Hanging the suit on the door frame, I fired up the computer.

First on the agenda the cash card and credit cards. I had suggested we have the joint account but he had argued against it, once the funds entering his account had dried up he had been more than happy to take the spare cards to my account I had offered him.

Well, let's see how well he coped without access to the money tree. As I chopped each branch away from under him, I felt satisfaction at the thought of his free fall into financial limbo.

Next the mortgage, it was due out in a couple of days, damn him if he thought I was going to pay for his half of the house. As I called the bank to cancel the direct debit, I contemplated how long it would take before the realisation of his stupidity hit him.

Would he realise before the letter landed on the mat announcing his arrears in blood red lettering?

The meeting lasted longer than I had anticipated, so I was starving by the time I left work. I thought about my half of the kitchen, the thought of trying to create anything edible with the microwave did not appeal. I dug my mobile out of my bag and called the Chinese, ordering my favourites to collect on the way home.

I looked at my watch, still time to make one more call.

I sat at my half of the table eating noodles from a paper plate. He sat opposite me just watching, I glanced over towards the washer expecting to see it empty. I had fully expected him to cross the line ad turn the water back on while I was out, but the washing still sat there, dried suds crusting the porthole.

The sound of an engine and clanking chains outside alerted me that the next blow was about to descend.

I watched his eyes widen as a veil of understanding settled there. I waited for him to react, but the only change was the tightening of his jaw. I wondered how he was managing to stay planted firmly in his seat knowing his beloved car was being towed away.

I picked up my plate and threw it in the bin, I could get used to this, no washing up. I grabbed a bottle of wine I had picked up from the shop next to the takeaway and a plastic glass and headed up to my room.

As I closed the door I heard him break down, a torrent of profanities unleashed before the outpouring of tears. I stuck in my earphones and turned up the music on my I-pod, I unscrewed the bottle and lay back against the pillows, glass in hand and lost myself in the music.

Tuesday

His eyes were puffy as I entered the kitchen. For a moment it looked like he was about to speak, but then he thought better of it.

I headed off to the gym again, I didn't need to be in the office till later today, so a soak in the jacuzzi after my work out occupied my thoughts.

After stopping off for a bagel and coffee for breakfast, I called in at the letting agents. Three properties were available for immediate let fully furnished. I made an appointment to look at the one I thought suited me best for that teatime, then headed off to work.

It was a long day mentally, it seemed I was surrounded by idiots. The simplest of tasks seemed beyond them as a result I was flustered by the time I reached the viewing.

It was perfect, the person who had decorated it obviously shared my tastes. The decor was subtle, allowing for the decorations and accessories to impose a person's own character, without compromising the design. I saw no point in delaying things and signed on the dotted line.

Friday would be moving day.

My mind raced with the possibilities for my new life. I planned the dinner parties I would throw and the people I could invite. I would be able to have who I wanted round without having to worry about being shown up by his ignorance.

As I headed home I called to have the gas and electric shut off. I told them we were moving, as I was the person who paid the bills they never questioned it. The gas would be shut off tomorrow, the electric on Thursday. I made a mental note to buy candles and a torch for my final night in the house.

I was literally bouncing with excitement as I entered the house until I saw him. I almost waivered.

He sat slumped at the table. Unwashed and unkempt, looking like a wreck, I longed to still go to him, to forgive him, maybe if he had spoken, I might have relented, but he sat staring at the coffee cup in front of him. Black coffee, his milk supply had obviously dried up.

I realised I hadn't thought about what I was going to eat, I pulled out the faithful mobile and ordered pizza.

"Please, will you just leave."

I looked at him. His voice sounded strained as if the very effort of speech had used every ounce of energy in his body. I considered my answer and walked to the dining room in silence.

I spent the evening in my room crossed legged on the bed, laptop open, ordering the necessary items for my new flat. Sheets, cushions, decorations to put my own stamp on the place. I heard him go to bed, I waited until I heard the soft rumble of his snoring, then crept downstairs.

I moved as stealthily as any thief through the living room, gathering a few items, which I felt I had the right to take, I had bought them after all.

I looked at the huge vases filled with decaying flowers, I normally replaced them long before they started to wilt. Now, they hung their heads in shame, pathetic, useless, past their prime, no use to anyone. I turned away from them in disgust.

I took the few items I had selected and took them back to the bedroom, I concealed them in a large holdall. I would take them to the office tomorrow and hide them there until Friday.

I gathered an armful of clothes to deposit at the dry cleaners the next day and fell asleep dreaming of the future.

Wednesday

By now I was settling into my new routine up and out the door to the gym, workout, and shower before work. Stop off pick up coffee and a bagel on route. Eat out at lunch, pick up a takeaway on the way home. It was much like my life previous to my marriage if truth be told.

Of course, I missed the intimacy of having someone to curl up next to on a night, but once I moved out, that could be easily remedied. I had to be honest with myself, I was getting over him really rather quickly.

I was angry rather than hurt, just who the hell did he think he was, to think I wasted my tears on him. Yet part of me longed to see him on his knees, to hear him beg my forgiveness, admit he was a stupid arrogant prat.

Would I forgive him? Hell no, but I wanted to see him grovel.

I decided to finish work early today and headed back to the house. I had actually forgotten in my musings that I had had the gas shut off, and the chill in the house struck me as soon as I entered. He was back at the table now, duvet wrapped round him for warmth. I looked over at his half of the kitchen and surveyed the carnage.

He had obviously tried cooking, only to realise the cooker would no longer function. Open tins sat next to a pan, made impotent through the lack of flames. He must have, by now, used every plate, cup and item he owned. Without the water the dishwasher had been useless. He sat, surrounded by the possessions he had sought to deprive me of, all of which had brought him nothing but misery.

I sat at the table across from him, studying his face. He was beaten and he knew it. All it would take were a few little words from him and he could end his misery.

Okay, I wouldn't forgive him, but I would at least put him out of his misery, in that I would tell him I was leaving in forty-eight hours. But no, he sat there silently, too stupid to even admit defeat.

Maybe it was his male ego that held him back, should I be the bigger person and offer the olive branch?

"Anything you want to say to me?" I asked.

He shook his head and got slowly to his feet. He walked like he had aged thirty years, shuffling along bundled in his duvet. As he reached the door, he looked back at me.

"And to think I loved you."

It was little more than a whisper and he was gone. I heard the TV go on, turned up full blast to drown out the world.

I thought about those words, what had he meant? They had sounded like an accusation, how dare he!

Was he now trying to suggest after his behaviour that, somehow, I was the one at fault? That I hadn't loved him? That I was less than worthy of him. He had a nerve.

I had given him everything, he was an ungrateful S. O. B. It would serve him right if he rotted here in his own filth. I walked over to the plug socket and pulled out the freezer plug. It would be shut off tomorrow anyway, so may as well start defrosting it now.

I went upstairs to the spare bedroom, laid back on the bed and pulled out my laptop. I spent an hour working on some figures for work before switching tabs and catching up with some friends online.

Of course, I didn't answer them truthfully when they asked how things were going. There would be time enough for that once I was out of this hell hole and in my nice new flat. I had been thinking about this house since I saw the new flat, and it fell short in all departments.

The layout was all wrong, the rooms too small, I had never been able to transform it how I wanted it. He had been so unreasonable when I had suggested knocking out walls or changing the rooms round. Well, now he could change it all back to his cosy cottage look, I would finally have somewhere with style.

Contented I fell asleep.

Thursday

I awoke early the sound of smashing echoing round the house. I turned to look at the alarm clock, a blank display looked back at me. Obviously, the electric had gone off during the early hours, I looked at my phone, 5am, nearly time to get up anyway.

As I groped round in the dark trying to find the torch I had bought, I came to the conclusion that shutting off the electric had not been my greatest idea. Stubbing my toe against some invisible mountain I let out a yelp.

Finally, grasping the thin metallic tube I managed to find the switch and turn it on. A thin shaft of pale light illuminated the few feet ahead of me. I shone the light round me trying to gather the rest of my belongings.

I made a decision; I would not be returning to this house again. I could not imagine spending one more minute than necessary like this.

A crash from below. Judging by the sound a shattering glass it was either the TV or window that had gone. I wondered what the neighbours must think, whether they would come round, or call the police.

He had associated with them before we got married, but as I explained, as I made sure we slowly disassociated ourselves from them, they were really not the sort of people we wanted to have to acknowledge knowing in public.

On the left was a businessman, a little vulgar and common, but respected enough for that to be forgiven, were it not for his wife. The mail order bride as I called her, my husband insisted she wasn't, that she was actually some sort of doctor, but I didn't believe him, he could be so gullible at times.

To the right, an elderly couple, from whom the odour of mothballs could frequently be detected. She talked incessantly of the days she had been a debutante, young and pretty, at parties with royalty. To be fair, she had showed me a couple of pictures to back up her claims, but constantly hearing about them was tedious.

I thought it rather sad, looking at her, that the pinnacle of her life should have happened so early. it had all been downhill since then.

I concentrated now on the task at hand. I made sure I had everything of value, laptop, phone, and the various wires, I stuffed them in my gym bag. I swiftly sorted through the remaining clothing, a few bits joining the already bulging bag, the rest lay unwanted, abandoned, let him do what he wanted with them, like everything, they were replaceable.

As I struggled with the zip my eyes settled on my hand. The large diamond nestled against the elegant gold band. I slipped them off, weighing them careful in my hand. I slipped the diamond back on the opposite finger and rummaged through the bag for my jewellery box.

Opening it I retrieved a ring set with a cluster of smaller stones. This was the ring he bought me, he had thought it showed how wonderful he was, choosing a ring all by himself, despite my pointing out the one I wanted on numerous occasions.

I had worn this for a few days before replacing it with the one I wanted. At first, I just thought he hadn't noticed but as he slipped the wedding ring on it could not have escaped him, he had never even brought the matter up

I headed carefully down the stairs and towards the door. By the entrance stood a small table bearing a pile of mail, I leafed through it by torchlight, I stuck a couple of the letters in my pocket. Then, I placed the rings on top of the junk mail and left.

I was distracted all day at work, convinced there was something I was missing. Something I had forgotten or left behind along the way.

No one commented on the growing pile of my belongings in the office. Nor did they question why I remained as they left. I curled up on the plush leather sofa in my office and closed my eyes.

Final Disintegration

I did not sleep well. The sofa was uncomfortable, but more than that I couldn't shake a sense of something being wrong.

First thing I had the cleaner help me load my belongings into the car and I set off at soon as the letting agents opened to collect my keys. I stopped off at the local deli and collected a few items to tide me over until I had chance to shop tomorrow.

An hour later, coffee in hand, I surveyed my new home. I had a meeting this afternoon which required my presence at work but I had an hour now to sit and relax before jumping in the shower and getting ready.

I wandered round admiring my new surroundings. I had yet to see any of the neighbours but given the exclusivity of the address I was confident I would finally be with my type of people .

Reluctantly I got ready and headed back to the office. I had hardly entered the building when my PA accosted me with the announcement that there were two police officers waiting for me in my office. As I entered, they stood helmets clutched in their hands. They wore the grave expressions of those about to deliver bad news.

It seemed they had been called by the neighbours a couple of hours after I had left. They had been going out and noticed the smashed TV in the garden. On entering the policemen had found him hanging, they had tried to cut him down, but it had been too late.

After a slew of personal and impertinent questions they left, and my PA came in with a coffee and pained expression, she looked like she had been crying, although for what reason was beyond me.

She started by offering her sympathies, as if she thought I needed them. I told her clearly they were surplus to requirements, he had turned out to be just as big a waste of space as the others, and I had left him.

She started babbling about what a nice boy he had been, how well he had been doing at the company before I bought out the previous owner. I could see her pause and consider her words now.

She said how it had seemed such a good match, me older and more settled, him young and good looking, and what a shame it was he had struggled in his work, being so in love with me, it distracted him.

What a shame it was, when barely three months after the wedding, I had had to let him go. She understood, I couldn't show favouritism, and how hard it must have been for me to do.

I held my hand up, unable to listen to her drone on about him anymore. I told her I needed her to find me a company to clear out the house. Yes, clear it top to bottom, there was nothing there of value.

After she left the room, I picked up the envelope that the policeman had handed me, and emptied it on to the desk. Two gold wedding bands and the diamond ring along with a folded piece of paper.

I sat staring at it.

I knew what it said they had told me when they handed it to me. Just a few lines.

I picked up the phone and flicked through my phone book it only took a few minutes to arrange for the house to be put up on the market but in that time my hand strayed unfolding the paper.

Just a few lines

I am sorry I couldn't be the man you wanted. I loved you so much.

Please forgive me

yours always

xxx

Broken

Empty, broken beyond repair. I can no longer heal myself, as once I did, and have done so many times through the years. Inside I am dead, numb, immune to further pain, a mechanism developed through necessity.

I loved too much, allowed you to drain every emotion until there was nothing left to seep from my pores. I fought to make things work, even though you were determined to sabotage every effort, then you turned to attack with accusations, unfounded, unsubstantiated, designed to destroy everything you proclaimed to love.

It is no longer a case of too much water under the bridge, the tears overwhelmed it, crushed it with their weight and washed the shattered fragments away. There are no pieces left to be rebuilt.

You are sorry, sorry for your loss, sorry for your own pain, but cannot understand the pain you have caused. Because you cannot feel it, then it does not exist, you cannot understand the concept of cause and effect, because if you had, how could you have acted so, over and over again?

I cannot remember when the tears dried up, when I realised, I was fighting a battle I could never win.

Everything you said you wanted you were determined not to have, and then you turn and point the blame at me. I am to blame for loving you, for fighting for so long, for listening to my heart not my head, not walking when I was strong.

I eat and sleep but do not feel, the risk is far too great, to open up, let down the walls and know I face defeat.

You took the one you said you loved, and destroyed her word by word, now you do not like the husk that remains in her place, yet she is your very own creation.

What The Sleeping Hear

The noises were driving her mad. The constant steady bleeps from the machines, the relentless ticking of the clock.

She longed for a change of staff, at least during the shift changeover as they did their rounds, there was the distraction from the dark. If she could have moved her face, she would have smiled at the way they had stopped worrying about what they said around her.

It wasn't just the staff, her family too now no longer seemed to believe she could hear them, a few would be in for a shock when she figured out a way to persuade her body to wake up.

It was amazing what they had confessed to her believing she could not hear, or would not remember, or maybe she did them a discredit, maybe they were trying to shock life into her body.

Maybe that confession from her best friend, about the affair she had been having with her hubby, was a ploy to make her sit up and shout at them all, then they would confess the plot, and they would all laugh.

Stacey had sat on the edge of the bed and taken her hand, she sounded like she was crying as she spoke, but she did not feel any tears dropping onto her hand or anywhere else. She had apologised for at least ten minutes before she got round to actually saying what she was sorry for.

Stacey had always struck her as very prim and proper, an irony not lost on her as she listened to the details of a torrid six-month affair Stacey had been having with her husband.

Stacey had actually been the wife herself, only a couple of years ago, when she had caught her own husband with the barmaid at the local bar after a pool match. She had been the shoulder Stacey had cried on, before deciding to give her marriage another go.

She wondered if Stacey's husband Keith had any idea about what had been going on, she doubted he would have noticed at all. It was common knowledge to everyone that he had resumed his fling with the barmaid within a fortnight of being forgiven,

When she considered things, she was not particularly surprised by the confession.

Possibly it was the drugs they were pumping through her body to numb her pain that also dampened her emotions, or maybe deep down she had known for a while and had avoided facing it.

Well that was not quite true, she had suspected her husband was playing away, but she would never for one moment have suspected Stacey.

She had suspected his secretary, his bosses' secretary, the girl in the dry cleaners, but not for one minute her own friend.

She thought she might feel better if it had been one of the others, it would certainly be easier to deal with, and she was definitely more upset by her friends' betrayal than her husbands. She had wished that she could sit up and slap Stacey if for no other reason than to shut her up.

Why did she really feel the need to confess to so many details?

Okay, she understood, none of them really believed she could hear them, and the confession was simply a way to ease her own conscience, but really, she wondered if Stacey had pulled out a diary and was checking to see if she had missed anything, so thorough was her account of their treachery.

She believed Stacey might have carried on for hours, blubbing and apologising, in between accounts of romps, had her parents not arrived with the kids.

They had thought nothing of the tears, after all they thought it was natural a friend should shed a few under the circumstances, and she had imagined them all hugging each other.

She did know her hubby would not be happy to learn of her friend's confession.

He would hit the ceiling, first of course would be denials and protestations of innocence. Then he would panic about the financial implications, after all the money was hers and if anything happened to her it went to the kids not to him.

All he would actually get was the right to remain in the house, unless he remarried, in which case he would have to move out and it would be sold the profits going to the kids.

She mentally gave herself a slap, she was thinking as if she were never going to wake up.

Her dad had been insistent on the will being made, alongside the prenuptial agreement, she had argued but it had been her husband who persuaded her to sign. She had boasted to everyone that it was proof of his love for her not her bank account, maybe in hindsight, that should have told her he only saw her as a stepping stone.

She could not actually remember the last time he had visited, had it been days ago. It was so hard to estimate the passage of time, but she was sure it had been at least a week since she had last heard his voice.

She even wondered if she actually wanted to wake up. Maybe it would be easier to just stay here in the dark. Okay, she was bored stiff, but at least she would not have to face her father and admit he had been right about the man she had fallen for.

She knew he would resist the urge to say 'I told you so' straight out, but he would take over. He would want to deal with the situation for her, and she was not sure she wanted that, but there was no rush.

She had plenty of time to think about it while she lay here.

The door opens and she hears two sets of footsteps entering, one set she recognises, and one new. She has no idea what the people really look like, but in her mind, she has created images for each individual, based on the way they move and their voices.

The footsteps she recognises belong to the nurse she has decided is pretty but plump.

The woman speaks with a soft voice and makes her think of a high school prom queen, not the real prom queen, not the girl that was part of the in crowd but the girl who everyone was friends with.

She would have been on the decorating committee and spent hours decking the hall before the others arrived. She would be pretty, but not stunning or so beautiful, she would be intimidated by others, completely unaware that she had retained her prettiness while their looks had faded.

She had labelled her plump merely because the woman was a little heavy footed. She knew it was possible she was being judgemental, but, lying flat on your back, unable to move and locked behind your own eyelids, the only thing you could do to try to maintain your sanity, was use your imagination.

The two had stopped moving, and she knew from the number of footsteps they had taken they were only just inside the room. She had counted frequently the number of steps from door to bed, bed to sink, door to window, and knew they had barely taken enough to allow the door to close after them.

"You sure she can't hear anything?"

It was a man's voice, deep and gravelly, it was not anyone she knew, not a member of the medical staff that had been here before and certainly not family.

It was a voice that a bad guy in a Bond film would be proud of she decided, immediately assigning the physical attributes of a villain to match the voice.

"No, she is in a deep coma, has been for months. Really sad case, they say her husband pushed her down the stairs, he insists she fell.

Unless she wakes up, I guess no one will ever know what really happened, he is out on bail at the minute, and their kids are with her parents."

Months? Had it really been that long?

Momentarily she allowed her mind to wander, trying to discern when people had last visited and make sense of the fact it had only seemed like a week or two at most had passed.

The man's voice pulled her concentration back to focus on his words.

"Tonight, it has to be tonight…"

"But I can't do it, I told you, I can't do it and even if I could, I am never alone to do it."

"All you have to do is open the door, at one AM, open the door to the ward and allow the janitor in, he will take care of everything."

"But they will know that we don't need one, that nothing has been ordered, a janitor would only come during the night if called for an emergency, please it won't work.

Please, I don't want to know what's happening or why, just please not here, they will know, and they will know I opened the door, that I am involved."

"That is not my problem, you owe my boss a favour, and he is calling it in, you open the door and keep your mouth shut, if not then you will be next."

The last words contained more menace than she had ever believed possible, his footsteps confident as they left the room. The nurse remained silent, her breathing barely audible, then with a sigh she too left.

The woman lay trying to make sense of what she had heard, tonight, she did not know if that was an hour away, or ten times that, time had lost all meaning, and what could she do?

Could she decide to wake? Could she force her eyes to open? And if she did would anyone listen and believe her?

Easier to stay here and pretend she heard nothing, pretend her loving husband would be visiting, pretend all was well with the world.

The Black Sheep

She had always known she was different, looking back through the family album, her otherness was accentuated by colour schemes. There she was, dark-haired, dressed in blue, flanked by angelic blonde cherubs, perfect in pink.

She pushed the picture away, sliding it beneath the pile of papers sat on her desk.

This was a ritual she had replayed many times, eventually the photo would re-emerge from within the pile, and she would take it up, examine it once more, before consigning it to oblivion back deep within the stack.

She looked down at the envelope that sat before her, heavy cream handcrafted paper, suggesting no expense had been spared, yet she knew better.

Her parents had trained her sisters well in the art of pulling a fast one, no doubt the poor printer, who had spent his time and energy creating these luxury invites, would find himself battling away in court for the next twelve months trying to recoup enough money to cover his costs.

She didn't need to open it to know what it was, though she had distanced herself from her family, distancing herself from hearing about them had proved impossible. Especially as they themselves were determined to claim their relationship with her, no matter how many phone calls were refused.

Of course, it hadn't always been that way, growing up she performed the role of unpaid servant, babysitter, cleaner and general drudge.

A shudder passed through her as she contemplated what her fate may have been, had a teacher not spotted the potential, and aided her in formulating her escape route. She had taken her after school one day to see the solicitor who had helped her secretly conspire to escape her own life.

She knew just how lucky she had been that all the right people had come into her life before it had been too late.

She had become emancipated from her parents age 15, after her teacher, had quite literally, threatened them that several aspects of their way of existence would interest various parties if they did not agree. A wry smile crossed her lips, when people talk of divorce, they always assume that it is the end of a marriage, but in her case her divorce had been from her nightmare family

Her father had been furious, he had ranted at her that they would lose the money that she added to the benefits total each week, that she was taking food out of her sisters mouths, he had tried every trick in the book to guilt her into backing down.

He had shown up at the school and shouted at the teacher until she had made it clear she would not be intimidated and had threatened to call the police.

It had been the thought of losing his liberty, and worse, having to pay back years of fraudulently claimed money, that had changed his feelings on the matter.

Not once, in all the arguments, could she recall emotion ever featuring in the rows against her gaining independence, not from their side at least.

She had owned only the clothes she had stuffed into her rucksack on the day she left the house for good. That had been the day she knew the summons was being served, demanding they attend the family court, up to that point they had not believed she would go through with it, more proof if it were needed they had really not known her at all.

She had stayed with the teacher and her family for the last few months of school and the first year of college before they helped her get her own place. It had been hard, she had worked two jobs, as well as studying, determined not to let down that one person who had faith in her.

Six years later it had been the teacher who had stood, proudly snapping photographs, as she graduated university, though her biological family had shown up hoping to help themselves to some freebies.

She had stood in the hall and flushed with embarrassment, listening to their voices protesting outside as they were refused entry for not having a ticket.

She had known that it was only the beginning, if she wanted a future, wanted to be successful then she had to realise they would attempt to spoil it at every turn.

Move forward a few years, opening night of her first play, they had once more descended upon her, despite the fact her sister had sold the story of her childhood to the tabloids the week before the curtain went up.

Actually, she had to admit, she had thought she was the only writer in the family, the only creative one, but she had to give her sister credit for the imagination she had applied to recreating their formative years.

She had kept her head down, smiled at the people that mattered, and ignored the fact they were trying to show her up, until their behaviour ensured the theatre's management had discreetly removed them.

The play had been a success and she had made enough money to pay them off. She had paid them to sign an agreement that they would not contact her, or try to profit from their association with her, in return, she had bought them a house, paid for in full.

The conditions stated, that should they break the contract, they would forfeit the house. She had come close to calling her lawyers on numerous occasions and having them thrown into the street.

It was a combination of a desire to avoid bad publicity, and the fact that so far at least the contract had kept them from actually showing up to harass her in person. They did not seem to comprehend that begging letters, invites to family occasions she had no desire to be part of, constituted a breach of the agreement.

She wondered what angle there was for them in this invite.

They knew better than to try to get her directly to foot the bill for anything, though of course they had tried over the years.

There was always something that they felt she should help out towards, the car had broken down, they felt she should buy them a new one. The arrival of nieces and nephews signalled an invite for a christening, along with a list of acceptable gifts.

The gift lists had always made her laugh, as she had yet to meet a new-born that needed a 60 inch 3D television or the latest games console.

That was the only time she ever felt a little guilty, the children had done nothing to her, yet she knew that if she gave in just once, the floodgates of requests and demands would follow.

Instead, all the children's birthdays and Christmas presents were the same, a fifty-pound gift voucher, which she had no doubt the children would never get the benefit of, but it eased her conscience.

It could be a 'photo op' for the highest bidder, they had actually done that before, at the wake for her grandmother. Only when the pictures of her, with tear tram lines down her cheeks, appeared in the tabloids the next day, did she realise just how low they would sink, but of course no one would admit to anything.

The ones at the graveside, anyone could have taken, but the ones of her leaning in the coffin at her grandmother's house, no, only someone invited into the house could have taken those.

She toyed with the corner of the envelope, tempted to open it just for curiosity's sake, then in a decisive motion she threw it across to the desk opposite hers where her assistant sat watching with a bemused expression.

"Reply, tell them I am out of the country and unable to attend, send something mid-price from the wedding list."

"And if you're not out of the country?"

"Make sure I am!"

She opened the screen back up on her computer and began typing.

She had it, the title for her new play 'The Black Sheep' after all who said being the black sheep had to be a bad thing?

Sometimes divorcing your family was the beginning, not the end, if only she could work out how to stop the flock following her, then she would be able to relax.

TABLE FOR ONE

A look of pity had flitted across the waiter's face as she had requested the table for one. She had smiled back at him, hoping to convey her contentment at her request.

He had seated her at the very back of the restaurant, in a corner, as if she had some contagious disease from which the other diners must be protected. She wished she had gone to her usual place, but she had her reasons for the change of location today.

Of course, it had not really been a table for one, but set for two, one place setting hurriedly removed as she took her seat. She picked up the menu and glanced at it, not really needing to study it in-depth, she already knew what she would order, she had thought about this often.

Catching the waiter's eye, she ordered her food and a glass of chardonnay before retrieving the book from her bag and flipping it open to the bookmarked page. She knew she would not read much, but still, it provided the barrier she required to enable her to people watch in peace.

She watched the families sat round the bigger tables, no children present here to require mummy's service as food dissector, only adult children sat with aged parents, possibly celebrating a special occasion, a wedding anniversary perhaps?

Then she allowed her eyes to drift along the couples. So many sat in silence, and she wondered how the waiter could pity her more than them. She was here alone by choice, well in some respects at least, they sat in pairs, but were more alone than she could ever be.

Her drink arrived and she took a deep draught from the glass, maybe a little too much too quickly, but she did not really care. The starter was delivered to the table and she was surprised how much she found herself enjoying the food, for a moment she almost forgot her reason for being here.

As the waiter cleared her table she ordered another glass of wine, she considered ordering a bottle but restraint was the order of the day, for now at least, and if she were honest there was something that seemed distasteful about ordering a full bottle for just herself, she felt as if the staff would judge her,

The main course arrived and as she ate her mind wandered to the meals she had prepared over the years, the loving care she had imparted into each and every one. Had they tasted better than the food prepared by a faceless chef hidden in the recesses of the building? Maybe not, but they had been no worse, merely different.

Her eyes kept moving to the watch on her wrist, it was nearly time, she was almost tempted to leave now, unsure she could go through with her plan, but then she saw the door open, and it was too late.

The woman walked in first, she had to be honest, she was not what she had expected, but then, what had she really though she would see, a painted whore?

No, this woman looked normal, she looked like in another world they would be friends. Maybe she was a little more polished, her hair was obviously straight from the stylists, and where as she had always had to copy style as best she could on a limited budget, she would make a bet that this woman's clothes bore all the right labels.

She lifted her book again and from behind its cover she watched as a couple were seated in the centre of the room. It was obvious that the woman was deeply in love with the handsome man who held the chair out for her as she took her seat.

She watched as the man at the centre table ordered for himself and his companion, she wondered if he knew the woman's favourite dishes, or if he was just ordering what he thought she would like to eat.

Her own memories of awkward silences as dishes were placed before her, dishes she had not asked for and had no desire to eat flooded over her. She looked down at the food in front of her now, knowing that this was still not exactly her choice, but it was at least a choice she had been able to make.

She forced a few more mouthfuls down, though she no longer felt like eating, but she did not want to offend the staff who had prepared the food, her loss of appetite was not their fault. When she had eaten enough for it look acceptable, she placed her knife and fork on the plate.

The restaurant was filling up now but she was thankful that her view remained unrestricted, the waiter returned to clear her plate. He enquired had everything been to her satisfaction, she had responded politely, made comments about saving room for dessert, a knowing smile passed between them.

She had been about to order another glass of wine when she changed her mind and ordered the bottle, she did not have to drink it all but the first two had hardened her determination to carry forth her plan.

The starters for the table she was watching arrived at the same time as her dessert, she looked down at the chocolate creation on the plate in front of her and thought, how under other circumstances, she would have enjoyed taking her time, savouring the decadent luxury. She raised her spoon to her mouth and for a few seconds allowed herself to indulge in the fantasy before she turned her attention back to viewing the couple sat centre stage.

In between mouthfuls of dessert, that were becoming increasingly difficult to swallow, she watched the man at the centre table as he spoon-fed his companion morsels from his plate. She pushed her plate aside and caught the waiter's eye motioning for the bill. As she waited for it, she poured one last glass of wine from the bottle, she sipped at it, steeling herself for what she was about to do, and wondering what the reaction would be.

The waiter placed a small leather wallet on the table in front of her, she let her fingers linger only briefly before catching the edge and flipping it open. She looked down and smiled, she had ordered the most expensive items on the menu and knew that it was an indulgence which would have been denied her had she been sat at that centre table.

Years of scrimping and saving, always grabbing bargains, so he could invest for their future.

She placed her book back in her bag and pulled her coat on, then rising to her feet she walked confidently towards the couple, now lost in each other's eyes. For one minute she paused feeling uncertain, years of loyalty battling against the urge now for justice and retribution.

They did not register her at first, only when she called out to the waiter did she fully gain their attention. She could see the look of panic on his face, the woman merely looked at her amused, totally oblivious as to what was going on.

She placed the bill in front of the man, and turning to the waiter, said with a smile and in a bold voice

"My husband will pay my bill!"

She slid the wedding ring from her finger and dropped it onto his plate, it landed with a satisfying splash in the gravy, and she felt exhilarated by the idea of the freedom her action had just afforded her.

At first the only noise she heard was her heels clicking on the tiled floor as she turned and walked away, the other diners sat stunned by the scene they had just witnessed, then the murmur of whispers began. She had just reached the door when she heard the shrill voice of another woman betrayed, the one who had never known she existed. She glanced over her shoulder just in time to see the wine fly from the glass into his face.

She stepped out onto the pavement and realised the sun had come out, it was going to be a lovely day after all, well for her at least.

Disintegration & Other Stories

Karma in Oils

I exhaled, the smoke drifted away as the stub made contact with the ground, before being well and truly extinguished by a perfectly placed stiletto. My head fell back, and for a moment, I regarded the night sky, and wondered if anyone would notice if I bolted right now. I had done the meeting and greeting, and polite small talk.

An evening of smiling, putting on my professional mask, when all I wanted to do was head home and cry into another bottle of wine. Then after drinking it, fantasize about wielding it, imagine the...no I was not to think like that.

Why is it so wrong for the woman scorned to display jealousy, though personally I thought of it more as pure anger, beautiful maliciousness?

Now my art had become my revenge, and tonight, I would send it out into the world so everyone would know, well I would, and he would, though I had made sure he was not too recognisable for the sake of the children.

I couldn't put it off any longer, if I did not reappear my agent would come looking for me, with well-meant words that generally made me want to scream. The icy blast of air conditioning hit me as soon as I entered, along with the overpowering stench of too many fragrances contained in one room. Stickers announcing sales were appearing on more and more paintings, my agent had a grin across her face, I am guessing she had mentally clocked up her percentage.

The star of the exhibit, a substantial canvas of a couple engaged in a passionate moment, painted so that the viewer had the same scene I had witnessed through the heavy brocade curtains of a plush four poster bed, stood in the centre of the room. There had been much discussion, much interest, but no one had yet taken the plunge and pulled out their cheque book.

I noticed a man stood a little way off, looking at it, head tilted slightly, I moved to the side of him curious as to what he would say. I did not recall being introduced to him at any point during the evening so I hoped he would not know I was the artist; people are always more honest with a stranger.

"You know it is a little like voyeurism? You know you should turn away, the moment is so intimate, yet somehow, you can't."

Now he had spoken to me I dare not reply in case my voice betrayed me. Part of me wanted to tell him that was exactly how I had felt when I had first come across the composition, instead I nodded as if to encourage him to continue.

"I don't really get art, I don't understand all this modern stuff, but this, I get, it is what it is. Though I have to say, I have no idea how they come up with the price tags either, was at an exhibition last week where the wanted to charge $10,000 for a white canvas with a blue dot in the middle and a red line across the centre, I mean how does that work?"

He turned to face me now and held out his hand.

"Simon Charlesworth at your service, and you are…"

"The artist,"

I replied with a chuckle, no chance of getting an unbiased opinion now, but it amused me to see the relief cross his face that he had not said anything he had any reason to regret.

"And for what it is worth, I completely agree about modern art, and as for the prices, I leave that to my agent, I think an artist is the person least qualified at times to put a financial value upon their own worth."

He laughed loudly causing a few people to look round,

"Well I guess most of us have an inflated sense of our own worth, that's why we are always pushing for pay rises. But pardon me for saying, you don't look like the sort of woman who goes round doing a peeping tom act for inspiration, did you use life models to paint from? I mean do you actually get them to do it, or is it just from your imagination?"

How easy it would have been to tell the truth, explain how bad weather forecasted had prompted me to catch an earlier flight from a conference, how I had walked in to my own bedroom and this scene had been burned into my memory. The apologies that followed and promises, and my weakness in staying, partly for the children but partly because I enjoyed my lifestyle my marriage provided. The painting had afterwards a form of therapy to take my mind off things, I had done it in my youth before wifely duties and the children had taken up my time.

Now I looked round at the fruits of my labour and wondered if my husband had genuinely been sorry and more attentive how many of these canvases would be on sale right now. I become aware the gentleman was watching me waiting for an answer.

"From my mind and watching too many films I'm afraid, possibly combined with too vivid an imagination."

The answer seemed to please him and for a moment I thought he was about to walk away.

"And what do your friends and family think to your paintings, I can imagine they stir up conversation over the dinner table."

"Ah well, they are firmly divided into those that love them and those that really have no interest whatsoever, it was a friend actually who hooked me up with my agent, they liked a painting so I said they could have it, I had no idea they intended to show it to anyone else, next thing you know here I am."

I gestured round the room, and his eyes followed my lead taking in to rich and famous, busy guzzling free champagne and making sure they were seen by the photographer from a well-known magazine who was wandering around. For a moment we both stopped and watched as a couple of lithe reality stars posed glasses raised in front of a painting and I smiled with the satisfaction of knowing that the artwork would feature in the shot in the next month's issue.

"You seem as out of place here as me, I am guessing you would rather just be able to do the painting and leave it to your agent to sell them?"

"You got me. However, it has to be done, for the paintings to sell you have to sell your soul alongside them, though to be honest, I think I sold that a long time ago. No, I shall smile and do my duty, make small talk with people I have nothing in common with, oh please, do not include yourself in that, you have been a blessing, I was considering making a break for it before I found you looking at this painting,"

"You know what, I think I am going to get this for my office. What is it called?"

"*The Adulterer.* Where do you work?"

"Congress, might not be appreciated by everyone, but certainly will be a conversation starter. Tell you what, you snag us a couple more glasses of champagne, while I go take care of the money before someone buys it out from under my nose, then you can tell me more about the life of an artist, and who those people in the picture are."

He moved off to my agent and I started to smile, my husband's infidelity would become a talking point in the very place he worked, and he would be unable to say a word.

DEUCE

It was her friend Donna, who first suggested the game of 'Mixed Doubles'. She had expected her boyfriend to decline he was not a big fan of tennis but Steve had responded with a great deal of enthusiasm and she had been elated he was taking an interest in something she enjoyed for a change.

That had been two weeks ago, before she had read his texts, she had not said anything, though it had been hard, but she was determined to make sure when she acted it would bring his world crashing down around him.

Somehow on the drive to the court it had changed into boys versus girls, power against skill, and though she was a little disappointed she hid her feelings. Smiling, two pairs of best friends facing each other across a court for a friendly game of tennis, how better to spend a couple of hours on a sunny afternoon?

They had decided they would not play sets, rather they would play first to win eleven games would win. The losers would buy lunch for the winners, she had smiled again, laughing along as they headed out from the locker room, the other three chattering away. They were throwing around the idea of them going away for a long weekend together, but she did not join in, she knew that was not going to be happening, not after today.

She and Steve had got together first, from there he had introduced her best friend Donna to his, Richard, and it had been the perfect set up. They double dated a lot at first, but life had got in the way recently, she had been promoted at work which had meant longer hours and working alternate weekends.

She hadn't minded the extra hours; they were saving for the deposit on a house. It had been his idea, the money they saved not going out on the weekends she worked, should go into a savings account for that purpose, but she had added extra in as well, hoping to speed the process up, what she had not done was check the balance regularly.

Her world had changed the day she picked up his phone instead of her own to send a text. She had never checked his phone, never felt the need, and there had never been an issue of using each other's phones. Hers was plugged in to charge upstairs, as she picked his up and typed in the code to unlock it, she had no thoughts of him possibly having anything to hide.

As she opened the text app her world spun, at first it was the name and one line of text that caught her eye, but then, once she tapped on the screen, there was no mistaking what she was reading. Quickly she had closed the screen and replaced the phone. She had had to fight back the urge to scream and shout and confront him there and then. She wasn't sure what was stopping her.

Instead she ran up and grabbed her own phone from the stand, he was just coming out of the bathroom, towel wrapped round his waist from the shower, she raced past him grabbing her bag off the bed and shouted over her shoulder that she was just running back to the office, that she had forgotten something.

The boys had won the toss and had elected to serve first, so far, they had all held serve once, making the score four games to three. This was what she had been waiting for, she had waited until her second time to serve, using the first to warm up, get the speed of the court and bounce of the balls measured ready for the precision shots she intended making.

She would show them they were the fools thinking they could play her.

She stood and looked across the court at her boyfriend who stood smiling back at her. The smug bastard, she thought, he doesn't have a bloody clue I am onto him.

She had not actually lied as she left the house that night, she had run to the office, she knew it would be empty and she would be able to sit and think. That was when she had checked the bank account, there was money there, just not as much as there should have been, the only money that remained was the extra she had deposited.

The money he had been putting in had gone in only to be transferred back out a few weeks later along with the money he knew she had put it. Obviously he had not checked the balance, or he would have seen there was more money there, she guessed she should be thankful for that and transferred the remaining funds back to her own account, leaving a single pound in to keep the account open so he would not realise she knew what was going on before she was ready to act.

She threw the ball high into the air, brought her racket round in a perfect arch, and stuck the ball like a missile straight towards him. She watched as it bounced just in front of him and he attempted to move out of its path. He failed miserably and the ball bounced up hitting him in the stomach.

Those years spent perfecting her serve with a tennis coach on Saturday mornings when she had really wanted to be hanging out with her friends were about to pay off, she made a mental note to thank her parents later.

15 – Love

She smiled as she called the score.

'Sorry sweetie are you okay?'

She had to make a conscious effort to sound concerned and stop the smile that was forming on her lips.

He stood up winded, nodding in response to her question.

She bounced a new ball on the ground in front of her before delivering an easy serve to Richard, that was her only regret, that he was mixed up in all this and had no idea what was about to go down. He returned it over the net towards his girlfriend, a nice easy shot that under other circumstances, she would have left to her teammate. She pretended not to hear Donna call that she had it. She rushed as if to hit the ball and clattered into her friend sending her sprawling to the ground.

'Oh, sorry hun, look how clumsy I am today. You're not hurt are you?'

She reached down to help her friend up noting with satisfaction the grass stain on her friend's perfect white skirt. As she jogged to the side of the court to retrieve the ball, she also noticed the quick glance between the two people she should have been able to trust the most.

15 All

She faced her boyfriend again he seemed to have recovered now from her first serve to him. Again, she gave the ball a bounce, testing its spring, before tossing it high in the air. She did not strike it as hard this time, delivering the ball to his weaker backhand, knowing he would slice it back towards her.

She chipped the ball back over the net and watched him scramble to get his racket to the ball sending it high into the air. She leapt up arching her back, swinging the racquet with all her might and smashed the ball straight at his head.

Steve staggered with the impact, but remained on his feet, just, if she was honest that disappointed her a little, she had hoped to knock him off his feet. Out of the corner of her eye she saw her friend move forward, an involuntary gesture, taking two or three steps before realising what she was doing and resuming her place on the court.

'Damn, my game is all over the place today, you okay babe?'

This time the tone of amusement in her voice could not be hidden, but Steve merely nodded, though she was sure she heard him muttering something beneath his breath.

15- 30

She waited while Steve cleared his head, feigning concern as he staggered towards the base line. She had hated giving the point away but there was a bigger game to be played today, and though it went against her competitive nature, she knew it could not be helped. She served an ace towards Richard, not wanting to risk hurt him, after all, he was not to blame for this farce they were being subjected to.

30 All

Facing her boyfriend again she sent him an easy serve this time, she knew she could not keep using the same tactics and it was time to switch it up, plus, she did not want the game to be over too quickly. He returned the ball to Donna, back and forth they hit the ball as if they were the only two people on the court. She waited patiently knowing he would not be able to keep control of the ball for long.

Eventually he returned it to the centre of the court, and she took her moment snapping her racket back and connecting. Donna fell to the ground as the racket connected with her nose with a satisfying crunch. Both the guys rushed round the net as she offered fake apologies.

She stifled a giggle as her boyfriend was pushed aside by Richard, anxious to comfort his girl. She grabbed a towel and water bottle and handed them to Donna who was trying to staunch the trickle of blood from her nose.

Her boyfriend was chastising her for the accident, she did her best to look innocent. When he suggested scrapping the game, she felt a flutter of panic that maybe she had let loose too early, but Donna clambered to her feet insisting she was fine to continue.

A look passed between the three of them, only Richard remained unaware of what was going on.

30 -40

She quickly served another ace to level the points and give herself a minute to think about her next move.

Deuce

Her next ace wrong-footed Steve and she had the satisfaction of watching him over extend and go flying along the floor. The tension on the court had increased but there was nothing he could call her out on this time. The looks between Donna and Steve across the court were more blatant now, and she wondered how Richard was not noticing them.

Advantage girls

She glanced down at her watch as she bounced the ball, right about now her parents would be at the flat with the removal van. Even if the game ended now, by the time they had showered and changed and driven back home the deed would be done, not that she had any intention of returning to the flat.

She sent a miss hit serve towards Richard and allowed him to return a winning shot.

Deuce

She launched another ace wondering how long she should keep this up for, she knew she could control the game all afternoon if she chose to. It was handy she had never mentioned to any of them she had played at Wimbledon as a teenager before a fractured wrist had taken away that dream. She could not help think karma had stepped in by allowing this particular skill to provide the exit from this nightmare.

Advantage girls

She was just about to serve again when Richard caught her eye,

'Hey, it's my serve next I want in on the fun.'

He winked at her as he called over the net. She served another ace.

Game

She waited watching as Richard served a high powered ball straight into his girlfriend's gut. Maybe this was 'Mixed Doubles' after all.

ONE LAST TIME

He stood at the door nervously clutching at the roses. Red, clichéd, a token but of what he was unsure. He rang the bell and waited.

She hadn't been expecting anyone.

Dressed in only her satin robe she answered the door and saw him. Instinct told her to close it, but she froze like the proverbial deer in the headlights. He took advantage of her surprise and moved past her.

He walked in and surveyed the flat. It was cold and stark, devoid of personality, so different from the home they had once shared. Guilt washed over him that it had come to this, he knew he was responsible, his actions had brought her here, but he could not change that, there was no point in dwelling on it any further.

Closing the door, she followed him into the living area. She did not question his reason for being here, though she had not expected him today, she had known that it was only a matter of time before this visit. Of course, he wanted to make sure she would agree to the divorce. The flowers threw her, surely lilies were more appropriate for the death of a marriage.

As she stood at the sink filling a vase, he watched her. He wondered how long it had been since he had really seen her. He saw her now, the girl he loved, had fought for, and won. Her figure was still trim, she had always been slim without being skinny, curves in all the right places, he had always retorted with pride when anyone had commented how lucky he was.

He had been lucky, she was always out of his league that was the irony, she was so clever and beautiful, he had not believed his luck when she finally agreed to go out with him. The sun shone in through the window, creating a halo around her head, and he felt dizzy looking at her.

Then he had thrown it all away, so carelessly and for what, a fumble, for a brief passionate encounter at a works party which had brought his world crashing down, and now trapped him.

He was talking but she is not listening. She can think of nothing she wants to hear from him any longer, no that is not true she thinks to herself, but the things she longs to hear would make her a bad person in her own mind, and she has suffered enough.

He is talking about everything and nothing at once, there is so much he longs to tell her, she was the one person he could always share his problems with, but no longer, and there is no one else he can be angry with.

She took a deep breath, steeling herself to face him. She could have forgiven his infidelity, but the child on its way changed all that.

He rose from his seat, drawn to the ghost of what had been, he knew he shouldn't, and fully expected to be rebuffed, but what was there to lose, he had already lost her. He was drawn on like a moth to a flame, instinct and longing replacing logic and thought.

One hand encircled her waist and pulled her close to him, her hands clutched to the worktop to stead herself, her mind raced but her reactions were to slow to stop the distance between them closing. The vase had slipped from her grasp tumbling back into the sink, water and roses tumbling out. His other hand had found her lips, silencing her, as his own fluttered butterfly kisses down her neck.

He whispered in her ear 'just one last time'.

She could feel her heart race despite her mind screaming this was madness. She felt powerless to resist as he turned her to face him and found herself looking at the man she had vowed to love forever. The past few months faded into the background, and all she could think about was the years they had been happy.

Lying lips locked over hers. She tried not to respond, her hands pushed against his chest but the effort was half hearted, more for show than a real desire to push him away. Her treacherous body had betrayed her, and nothing her heart and mind could say, could stop the need for him that coursed through her veins.

His wandering hands returned home, seeking out familiar comforts. He sought out her breast, caressing it through the silken fabric. Feeling the puckering nipple inviting a kiss. He lifted her now, carrying her to the table. Chairs kicked aside as he placed her gently down. Hands moved to her shoulders, sliding the robe down and back. Revealing her.

Knowing her own vulnerability, she hesitates for a moment but no longer. She should not be doing this. But why not? He is her husband still, 'just one last time' as she marks her territory with her nails into his back. She allows him to push her back. To lay her down, as he had so many times before, knowing exactly how to tease her flesh as his teeth graze against her nipple.

She grasps his hair pushing his head lower. Squirming as his tongue hits the spot. He lifts his head, and she tastes herself on his tongue as she reaches down for him. It is she who is the aggressor now. She pulls him into her.

Harder and deeper, he strives to climb inside her, become one again, recapturing what they lost. Then in one brief explosion, they no longer know where they each end and the other begins.

There is an awkwardness as they pull clothes back into place, once again he begins the small talk, but a look at her silences him. His train of thought lost in remembrance.

She does not feel empty, as she would have expected to, a part of her feels empowered, and she catches her reflection in the mirror, the wanton woman. Hair messed up, face and chest flushed and her eyes sparkle for the first time in a long time.

She does not want him back, she has no intention of forgiving or forgetting, at this moment she is unsure what she does intend, but in a strange way, this last time has freed her,

She returns to the sink and takes a minute to scoop up the roses and replace them into the vase.

Blood red roses.

She glances at her fingernails, and sees the colour mirrored beneath their manicured sheen. A smile crosses her lips as she thinks about the excuses he used with her, the lies he would tell, and wonders if he will use the same ones or if he has new ones now. She bites on her lip to stop the laughter pouring forth, of course, she would know where he had been when he showed up with the papers in hand.

She searches in the drawer next to the sink until she finds a pen, then turns and reaches her hand out to take the sheaf of papers from him.

His hand is shaking as he passes the divorce papers over, he does not want this, but knows he has no right to complain. He has ruined his marriage and now has the child to think of. He has forfeited consideration of his own emotions, and now must do the right thing. He watches as she signs with a flourish, and he cannot help but notice, she seems so much more confident now than she had when he arrived.

She reminds him even more of the woman he fell in love with rather than the shell he had turned her into. He thinks she must still love him, maybe there could still be a chance, and longs to rip up the papers as she hands them back to him. Then, she looks at the clock and dismisses him, claiming a prior engagement she needs to get ready for and the moment is gone.

After he leaves with signed papers in his hand, and the promise to call on his lips, she wipes down the kitchen table, and thinks how easy it would be to become the other woman.

Disintegration & Other Stories

Empty

She stood in the centre of the room, devoid of furniture it seemed cavernous, a stark contrast against the constriction of her stomach as reality set in.

The past few weeks had passed in a whirlwind no, that was not right, it had been a tornado, destructive, terrifying and had destroyed her world. It had left her stranded here now in a desolate no man's land.

Three months ago, she had been blissfully unaware of what lay ahead, leafing through holiday brochures, debating the perfect location for the holiday they both needed so badly. Their careers were both taking off, they were both spending long hours at the office which had seemed to be leading to them spending quality time together rather than quantity or that was what she had believed. What it had actually led to was guilt driven shows of affection compensating for the fact he was preparing to move on.

When they had met, he had already owned the house it made sense when after almost a year of dating that she gave up her rented flat and move in. She had begun investing in turning his house into their home straight away, her savings that she had been carefully squirreling away for a deposit to buy her own house now paid for the new kitchen and the renovating of the box room into an en-suite for the master bedroom. She had not thought twice about spending the money after all it was an investment in their future, he would occasionally talk of putting her name on the deeds but never got round to it.

She had redecorated room by room to show off the antique furniture he already owned; they had enjoyed days out on trips to antique markets searching out extra pieces to compliment the décor. Their tastes had complimented each other and occasionally he would come home and surprise her with the perfect picture for the room she was working on, her friends would tell her how lucky she was to have a guy that not only noticed what she was doing but cared enough to contribute. Within a few months she had given the whole place a fresh breath of air.

Looking back, she could see it he had been less enthusiastic than her about the whole process, he had been pleased with the results, but far less hands on during the process than she had thought he would have been. She had stripped paint from the woodwork, sanding and revealing the natural grain of the timbers late into the evening as she waited for him to get home from yet another late-night conference call. He would come in and slip his arms round her waist from behind and admire her handiwork, he would tell her how proud he was of her.

They would host dinner parties where he would boast about how talented she was; talk about the trips they had taken to pick up individual items. He would never correct them when they commented on the hard work it had taken, to restore the floor and doors to their original glory, assuming he had done the physical work, she would smile at him and remain silent allowing him to bask in the praise.

When had it began to stagnate she wondered?

After a year of living together he put a ring on her finger. It had been a public proposal at a family party with a ring that she had ended up keeping in the safe too valuable to wear on a daily basis, but he refused to set a firm date. He kept repeating there was no rush, they had the rest of their lives to spend together, he just needed things to calm down a little at work then he could make plans.

Time had passed and both of them were working hard, she had thought they were both making an effort to try to find more time for each other, but it had been hard. He had begun taking business trips that her own career prevented her from joining him on, but she had trusted him completely. The first few times there had always been a gift, some trinket for the house that suggested she had been in his thoughts during his absence, then he would have no time to look, or say he had not found anything suitable.

There were no rows, despite them both working long hours, after all they were both working for their future. She had suggested the holiday and been surprised how easily he had agreed they needed it, he had given her a couple of different sets of dates and left the rest in her hands his only criteria was that the hotel should have a spa, and she had laughed knowing that she already had the perfect place in mind.

Then the call.

Five years destroyed in less than five minutes. He had been too cowardly to even face her as he ripped her world to pieces. He had met someone… he was in love…moving in…selling the house…furniture going in storage… the fragments of the conversation punctured the disbelief she felt. He was sorry of course, but she surely understood, they had drifted apart and no point in dragging it out.

She had sat up all night waiting for him to come home. Angry, hurt and confused but not ready to give up their relationship without at least understanding what had happened and how long the betrayal had been going on. She had finally passed out in the early hours, still curled on the couch, the cushion soaked with tears. Mascara streaking the reproduction vintage fabric she had commissioned to compliment the curtains.

Then the second bombshell had dropped. A phone call the next morning, he wanted her out in a month. Not only was he abandoning her, but he was also discarding her and leaving her homeless.

He added insult to injury by reminding her it was his house and that she had no right to anything other than her own possessions, she wondered as she listened to him talk if he had checked his position already with his works legal department, he was talking about the money she had spent on the house being in lieu of her paying him rent over the previous years, he seemed to be deliberately ignoring the bills she had paid.

She had snapped at that point launching her own tirade of his failures, as the words flowed from her mouth she surprised herself with the venom she found she was capable of, she had thought they had been happy but now so many faults and issues seemed so obvious to her. Though she had sounded angry she knew she far calmer outwardly than she felt, she refused to be thrown out on the streets, she told would go once she could afford to. She needed time to gather money, she reminded him of the money she had spent on the house, pointed out she had paid for the kitchen and bathroom, he owed it to her to give her time, unless he wanted her to take them with her or he was prepared to pay compensation. That had silenced him, and the phone had gone dead.

He had returned a few days later while she was out at a work, she suspected he had been watching waiting for her to go out. He had taken all his personal possessions along with the most valuable antiques from the house. He had taken her engagement ring from the safe, along with numerous other items of jewellery, that had been a real slap in the face to her. She wondered how long he would wait before he slipped it onto another finger.

Two weeks after this the letter had fallen on the mat, the official notice of eviction from his solicitor and an appointment for the removal van to come to pack up and collect the contents of the house. She was to vacate prior to the removal with any personal effects she wished to take with her, she was supposed to turn in the keys to the estate agent, but she had not.

She had moved her things to her parents' house then on the day the removal men had arrived. She had sat across the road in her car tears flowing as she watched them carelessly cart out the items she had so lovingly selected. Once they had left, she had come back in and wandered from room to room, her footsteps echoing from the bare floorboards.

She could not believe his naivety that he had really believed she would go meekly, that she would accept his decision and he could go on with his life happily. She was already empty but soon that would be literal, she placed the envelope on the mantle where they had once been immortalised, smiling at sunset on a far-flung beach.

She took the knife from her bag and took off her jacket, she threw it where the chair had once stood and watched as it fell in a heap on the floor.

There was no hesitation, she had researched her subject thoroughly, prepared herself, after the first cut she had sat on the floor before making the second, then as she made the second she fell back into the pose she had calculated she would land in. As the blood flowed she felt a strange peace, and the cold, she had read about that but not expected it to be so tangible, her last thought as a smile formed on her lips was that he would have to live with this and she knew it would destroy him.

It did not take long before she was truly empty, the crimson life force spread around her sinking into the floorboards she had so lovingly sanded by hand and varnished.

The house gave a sigh, she was home, and it would never be truly empty again.

To be continued…

Author's Notes

This book was my first publication, coming about just after the end of an 18-year relationship. I already had many of the stories written and some had been published previously on my blog. Being single in my forties made be re-evaluate what my dreams were and how I could achieve them instead of trying to make others happy first, the result was this book.

About The Author

Born in Leeds, currently living in Huddersfield, Paula Acton is many things, an author, a mother to two amazing kids, grandmother to two gorgeous little people, and a slave to a dog, and a cat. She also has two horses which she claims are cheaper and more effective than therapy.

She has a tendency to write fantasy with a dark twist but also writes the occasional romance after success in various anthologies trying out different genres.

When not writing she can frequently be found wandering around randomly with her camera or with her headphones in listening to True Crime Podcasts.

You can find out more on her on her various social media sites

Website - http://paulaacton.co.uk

Facebook - https://www.facebook.com/Paula.Acton.Author

Instagram - https://instagram.com/paulaacton/

Twitter – https://twitter.com/Paula_Acton

Or you can support her over on her Patreon https://www.patreon.com/paulaacton/membership

Disintegration & Other Stories